PLEASE FORGIVE ME

Sola Olorunda

Please forgive me by Sola Olorunda

Copyright ©2018 Sola Olorunda

Please forgive me by Sola Olorunda

CHAPTER ONE

It was a sad day for Oye's family with the sudden death of their beloved son Wole. Wole`s death comes miraculously to everybody in that community No.4 Ayeniromo street Orunogbeke Avenue, this is where Dr. and Mrs. Oye lived with their two children Wole and Bose. They are lovely parents who care for the welfare of their children Wole and Bose loved themselves to the extent that hardly someone can know who is elder among them. It was only people that are closed to the family that can only know their position, Wole was the eldest while Bose was the younger.

Dr. Oye a medical practitioner who was famous among his colleagues from his diligent at working place. He was complete gentle man whom everybody loved both at home and working place, so also Mrs. Oye who is a Teacher in the nearby community, but she owned a shop in a nearby place not too far from their home she is a good mother to emulate when we talk about her dedication to the welfare of her children. The love both parent had for their children does not allow them to pamper them, they trained them in order to become somebody and prosper in the future. Wole and Bose attended the same school in their community, the only close friend they had was Tola whose parent also closed with Oye's family, and they are living in the same community but in the same street.

It was in the evening that the body of Wole was found in the swimming pool at the backyard of Oye's house where they normally played in their leisure period either after the school hours or during the weekend after they have returned from the school and ate their food, Bose and Wole slept off in the sitting room, only for Bose to woke up and called her brother name many times without any response, this led to a situation where by she was searching for nook and cranny of the compound when Bose could not find his brother, she ran to her mother shop to informed her about the incident that happened concerning the missing of her brother Wole, who they slept together in the sitting room. When Mrs. Oye saw her daughter she taught they had quarrel at home that was way Bose frown her face before getting to their shop. But it was a different story entirely for her. After Bose had narrated the whole story Mrs. Oye's Looked worried immediately about the where about of her son, people around the shop got to know through her reaction, when they asked her she told them what was going on somebody raised a question that who is Wole best friend so that they can go and find him there, probably whether he went there to played. Bose answered that it was only Tola that always be around with them at home, sometimes they came together from school and played before Tola leave to his house before day dark. But on this fateful day, Tola did not follow them to their house, but they agreed to check him at Tola house he might have woke up and go to Tola's house to play with him so far they are friend and their family are very closed and everybody knew.

Mrs. Oye and co-tenant in the shop including Bose they left to Tola's house to look for Wole on getting there they could not find him but they met Oye at home including his parent Mr. and Mrs. Ola the incident was narrated to them and they all agreed to go back to Mr. and Mrs. Oye's house to search very well for Wole, they believe that so far he was not with Tola may be he slept somewhere in the house that Bose did not checked because of her worried, when they got to Oye's house they checked every room in the house including the stone kitchen and toilet and bathroom, after through with that, they started checking the compound in order to know where he was, but to everybody surprise he was found in the swimming pool which he was already dead. Before Mrs. Oye living her shop to Tola's house she had phoned her husband to informed him about the strange missing of Wole their son, immediately Dr. Oye heard the news he took his car and rushed home to know where about of his only beloved son. He met them at home by the time they had discovered his body in the pool where he drawn, when he got there, he immediately order them to took him upside car to his private Hospital named Anuloju, when they got there all there effort was proved abortive and Wole was later confirmed dead. This was a shocked for everybody in that area because the boy was a gentle and easy young person.

The mystery behind his death cannot be ascertain at that moment because there was nobody with him before his death expect her younger sister that they slept together. Almost everybody was dumbfounded expect Bose who was continuously asking who killed my brother?

CHAPTER TWO

The sudden death of Wole the only son of Dr. and Mrs. Oye was a topic sentence in their community because when the sad news filters into the air everybody in that area troop to their residence for commiseration and condolence visit. Arrangement was made to bury Wole without the present of his parent to witness the burial of their child, in Yoruba Culture and tradition, colleagues of decease parent also present in their home including the staff of Dr. Oye and Mrs. Oye from her school.

The landlord association and neighbour in that area also present to pay a condolence visit to the family. The headmaster led the delegate from Wole's school to commiserate with them, Mr. Ayelari who was the headmaster comment on the sudden death of Wole who he described as the most brilliant in the school, he lamented that Wole was a role model among his students because of his exceptional displayed of a good character, he was the one to be chosen in the next academic session as a senior prefect because of his brilliant performance. It has been agreed among the management and Wole was also informed privately but yet to made public to the entire school.

Ogbonologbon primary school quiz master also commented, he was the head of literary and debating society of the school where Wole was the speaker, Mr. Otitoloju spoke and weep, he said Wole has delivered them time without members from many embracement during the debate with neighboring schools who wanted to defeat their school in many occasion. Wole was a good speaker who can stand and defend himself in any choosen topic for debate, he further said he could remember the day Orunogbeke primary school came from another state to compete with them, the speaker of that school was a good speaker as well and the prize to be won was very expensive, that is why both school try to carry the day. It was tough contest between them at the end of the day Wole beat his opponent to give the prize and glory to his school which everybody commend him and also reward with some special treatment. Game master also commented that Wole was the fastest boy in the school, he won the 100m race in many occasion and he was the anchor in school relay team. The class teacher cannot hold his voice as he said I lost my child even though Wole was not my biological son but. I used to call him my son because I told my children to emulate him he was a genius that emerged once in life time of one generation.

Landlord chairman Mr. Ayefele spoke on behave of other landlord. He comment that since he knew Wole as child of Dr. Oye he has never seen him quarrel with anybody in the area, he always teaches my son on subjects he did not understand which my son told me in many occasion, also his performance in debate also made my son happy because he always confident that whenever Wole was around they will surely emerge victorious in any contest. The Pastor in Dr. Oye church also present at their home, he described Wole as a rare gem who everybody we greatly missed including the entire church because of his responses to questions in Sunday school and other church programmes that involved questioning and answering, he was the best among his pupils. He later prayed for the family and enjoyed them to take heart and moved closer to God more than they do before, Pastor Olootoda also prayed to God to give them the fortitude to bear the loss.

Everybody leave the premises and left the other members of Oye's family stayed behind including Tola's parent because they were closed. In Wole's school a minute silence was made for him to pay tribute to a devoted fellow, the whole school mourn him and they agreed that he will greatly missed. After the assembly the Headmaster call for urgent meeting to resolve the changes that suddenly occurred in the school management including the former decision they have made. First on the agenda was the vacant position of Head Prefect which was given to late Wole Oye but due to his sudden death they need to bring another person to filled the vacuum. The school management resolved that the most brilliant must take the position and the second runner up in school was Tola who was Wole best friend because they always stayed together even he was the deputy Speaker in literary and debating society.

In that meeting Tola was chosen to replace Wole as a new Head Prefect in the next academy session. Immediately after the meeting the information was conveyed to Tola as a new head boy and also a new speaker for literacy and debating society. This development was not knew to everybody because Tola was the next person with good academic performance to Wole, So no doubt about his emergence as the new leader. He was extremely happy but, he cannot show it because of his friend sudden death.

CHAPTER THREE

Tola's parent could not hold their tears because of the relationship between them and Oye's family, they stayed with them and continue to console them especially Bose who always asked this question who killed my brother? It was a mystery for Bose because they slept together before she could not find her brother again until the reality of his death was later revealed in the pool. Tayo also was there to sympathize with the family of his best friend including Bose that was also closed to him. After few days when other family members have gone to their various destination. Dr. and Mrs. Oye took heart and back to their various place of work their conclusion was that Wole wanted to play in the pool and he eventually drawn which led to her death, but Bose disagreed with her parent in their conclusion, she said since they have been played around the pool, Wole has never swim because he hates swimming, he always discourage her not to go to pool to swim, with this only God knows! They console Bose and talk about another issues Bose found it difficult to stay alone even to the extent that she was always crying whenever she was alone, but Tola's parent has allow their child to stay with Bose sometime he slept in their house and from there they prepare for school which they always go together. Oye's family was always happy whenever they see both of them together because Tola was the one taking care of Bose both at home and in the school. Tola's parent always visit Oye's family not only to see their child when he was not at home but also to shows commitment and loyalty to them after the death of their child. During the long vacation period Tola stayed throughout in Oye's house only people that knew the beginning can only understand that, Tola was not Oye's son but, anybody that was visitor can never know what is going on. Dr. Oye always took them out together whenever he wanted to do shopping for her daughter so also Mrs. Oye did the same thing. The relationship between Oye's and Ola's family do everything together hardly would you see one in one place without the other.

When the resumption came Tola and Bose resume to school, Tola promoted to primary six while Bola promoted to primary five. Immediately they resume to school all arrangement has been made to introduce the new prefects to the entire school as usual. It was on the assembly that the coronation took place, this was excitement galore for those who has made the list of new prefect that would direct the affair of that school for the next academy section. The headmaster welcome everybody and addressed them that this was the new academic session, everybody should prepare themselves for new challenges including the staff and students, he continues today was our inauguration day of new leaders in the school, you must remember the traditions of this state that, anybody that was the best student in any school should be given automatic scholarship to the university education level, not only that, the best student male would be the head boy likewise the best student female would be the head girl respectively.

However, the headmaster continue his speech and introduction of the new prefects. It was a long awaiting day for everybody because those who emerged as Head-Boy and Girl, their parents would not pay any money or responsibility over them again, it was the duty of government to do that for them till university level and also produce job opportunity for them. The result of last academic session was announced and for male category Tola was emerged victorious and automatically became head boy, debate Speaker and also enjoyed state scholarship. In the female categories Eniola was emerged and also enjoyed the benefit like Tola. Everybody congratulate them including the other Prefects such the Assistant Head Boy and Girl, time keeper, Late comer Recorder, Janitor, Game Prefect, Social Prefect and so on. Head Master told everybody to be diligent and cooperate with the entire staff in other to be successful in their tenor.bose was not happy when the coronation was going on even when they started congratulate the new prefect, she kept mute and stare without talking to anybody, some notice her reaction they taught the sudden death of his brother was still in her memory, but they were all proved wrong by the time tola called her to let them proceed to home and bose told tola that if not the sudden death of my brother, he would have be the one to confirmed as head boy today and also enjoyed the benefit of scholarship, she concluded by saying who killed my brother! Tola looked at her fixedly and hug her, Bose you know the death of your brother pain everybody including I, but you supposed to be happy because that position was still within our reach, I am your brother best friend and also you are my friend now not only that the two family has been living together like one family, please forget about the past and let moved forward. They started talking till they got home. Tola did not stayed in Oye's house in that night, when he got home he narrated everything to his parent and they congratulated him for his success and also wish him best of luck, but at the back of their mind they knew they has been relieved for burden of responsibility on their child, since Tola informed them them in the last session that he was going to be the best student after Wole's death, they knew the scholarship was sure for him, because both parent were not financially buoyant enough to send their child to university, they always told their child to work hard in order to get scholarship from the government. Bose got home and told her parent what has happened in the school, she also told them what she did to Tayo and Tayo's response about it, her parent console her and told her to let them accept their fate.

Please forgive me by Sola Olorunda

CHAPTER FOUR

Tola started his position as the head boy in school, he was given free hand to direct the affairs of students. Literary and Debating Society Club was took another form by elected new members which Tola was the Speaker automatically because of his status as Head Boy. Deputy Speaker was elected and the Quiz Master always on ground to monitor what they are doing, he taught them some likely topics that can come out whenever they are preparing for debate. Tola school was the best in that state in term of Quiz and Debate and the responsibility was shoulder to him as they new Speaker. Many believe that, he would definitely save them from defeat.

It was a different stories for Ogbonologbon Primary School because the first time they went for debate they came second which has never happened to them. To many people surprise, but the management believe that victory not always comes in life. In the quiz competition they also lost the first position to other school in contention. The quiz master was not happy about the new predicament they found themselves but they still continue and do more rehearsal on many topic for debate and current affairs. Tola was not happy about the situation he found himself but his closed relationship with Bose continues because she was among literacy and debating society.

Throughout that session no honour or prize was won by Tola led Literacy and Debating Society including the Quiz competition. The management was not happy, but, they leave everything for God. Everybody in the school was not happy with the situation they alleged debate society not leading them to expectation, this statement was convey to Tola and he was not happy, he called other members of literacy and debating society and quiz competition for an emergency meeting. When they gathered, he told them what is on the ground and solution, everybody responded and agreed about the incompetent of their leader. Tola was sad to hear this but nothing he could do. Bose signified that she wanted to comment about the issue she lamented that if not the death of my brother this cannot happened to them, he was supposed to be the speaker. Who killed my brother! She concluded.

Tola could not comment further and he called the meeting to an end everybody departed. Bose did not wait for Tola before she left home and Tola looked for her to no avail, he also left to home. When Tola got home he narrated everything to his parent what had happened in the school and Bose comment about it. His parent concluded to call a meeting between them and Oye's family in order to resolve the nagging issue concerning their children. It was Oye's house the meeting was held and Mr. Ola narrated everything to Dr. Oye about her child comment in the public concerning the position of his child. Dr. Oye asked Bose to react to allegation that was leveled against her.

To everybody surprised Bose did not deny it, she repeated what she has said. This brought her father to conclusion that he needs to call her to order and mandated her not to talk about his brother again. He told her that what has happened God knew about it and they had accepted their fate.

Dr. Oye told Tola to take Bose as his sister and continue their family friend, Bose was asked to apologize to Tola and the issues was buried. The two family continues their relationship and friendship. Tola continues to look for Bose and she has no choice to adhere to directive of her father, she welcome him and continues to feel for him, when she remember what her mother said after Ola's family has gone that if her brother Wole was alive and what happened to Tola as a head boy happened to him what would you do? This statement made Bose to forget about the issue and has feelings for Tola predicament. At the end of the session nothing was won by Tola led literary and debating society including the quiz competition. In the closing ceremony at the end of the session. Head-teacher prayed for outgoing prefects and enjoyed them to work harder in their various college in order to improve on their future endeavour, they should put behind their poor adventure in primary school. They should pray to God for more wisdom and ask for forgiveness of any sins that could hinder their progress and success in life especially their future ambition.

After the Common Entrance the result was released and Tola proceeded to secondary school. And Bose promoted to primary six, she won the best female student and automatically qualify for head Girl including scholarship to university level. In the resumption day for new academic session, the head teacher welcome everybody and congratulated the new head boy and girl for their un relent effort to emerged victorious on the last academic session. He introduced them and urged them to redeem the image of their school who had lost the glory in area of academic performance such as overall best school, winning prizes in literary and debating society including quiz competition. The head boy Sola Olorunosebi spoke on behalf of others to put more effort in order to redeem the image of the school. Bose Oye the head Girl also promised them for total change.

The necessary arrangement was made available for the new prefects to succeed in their endeavour, they took advice from the management and work together for the progress of their school. To everybody surprise the image of the school was eventually redeemed and the lost glory was restored by winning every available medals and prizes in all literary and debating society including the quiz competition. The management was happy and gave kudos to Sola and Bose led regime. In the end of the year party head master on his speech, he gave glory to God almighty for wonderful miracle He did in that school about their glory and also prayed to God to guide the outgoing prefects in order to succeed in their future endeavour. Dr. Oye, Bose's father was on the valedictory service, he gave glory to God for wonderful performance of his daughter who God used to erased the sudden dead of her brother from his minds, he said what they did not allowed Wole to do, Bose has done it.

The ceremony was concluded.

CHAPTER FIVE

Tola continues his career at Reward Secondary School, he has already told Bose to choose the same school as the first choice, and fortunately she was admitted to that school. Bose and Tola continues their friendship likewise their parents, they did everything together, they both joined Press Club and participated in all activities involving social lives. They are always together which everybody knows. Their parents has already enjoyed the scholarship given to them by government, they spent nothing on them again. As time goes on Tola and Bose could not do without themselves.

Tola was passionate to be senior Prefect, meanwhile he has contested for Press Club president which he lost. The issue of Press Club president was the second highest office to senior prefect.

It was the second highest position in that college and only senior secondary school III student can contest for it.

This is student's affairs which none of the management interfere, they allow the students to choose their president by voting. Tola was one of the contestant, his friend's campaign for him including Bose who worked tirelessly for him to emerge victorious. The only candidate that contest with him was Lucky, Lucky was a brilliant student like Tola, they were always head to head in their academic performance. It was very difficult for school authority to choose the best among them. On the Election Day, they were 55 members of press club which everybody has a right to vote for their choice. The electorate was member of outgoing students.

By the time they finished voting they started counting and out of 55 votes Tola scored 17 while Lucky 38. When the result was announced. It was a shocked for both Tola and Bose because everybody believe Tola would win at all cost because he was a former head boy in primary school which

Lucky does not privileged to be. Bose was so sad likewise her friend that worked with her for the success of Tola in the poll.

Lucky was announced as the new President of Press Club and everybody accepted him. Activities continues in the school and the only vacant post which was also the highest office for a student was Senior Prefect, this office would be determine by the school authority.

They are moving closer to end of session and D-day was getting nearer. The principal Mr. Olorunosebi held the meeting with the management and top of the agenda was the issue of prefects especially the senior prefect. He posed the question to them by asking them that, who are they prefer to be the prefect and can they use the criteria they had been used before to pick the senior prefect. Some agreed some disagreed. Those that agreed were in opinion that so far the criteria has been used for long they should not change it. But those against said that, they need to change it, because of the situation on ground which they need to considered. The criteria was that overall best student with highest score in every subjects will emerged as the senior prefect this decision was favour Tola because he had 71% recorded while Lucky had 70%, those against argued that the margin is too slim to be used and Lucky is the Press Club president, it will be convenient for him to direct the affairs of the students as a Press Club President and Senior Prefect also the student voted for him to emerged which shows that they like him more than Tayo, if he can be selected all students will agreed with the management it will also bring more peaceful-coexisted between the students and the school management.

The principal appreciate everybody and kudos for their reasonable contribution he explained further that both side have a genuine reasons which they need to follow but he could not be in one side and leave the other side views, this will lead to element of bias, in this case they should emulate the students by voting among them in order to know the head that wear their crown. The voting commenced out of 48 staff including teaching and non-teaching staff Tola got 23 votes while Lucky got 25 vote. Eventfully the matter was laid to rest and lucky emerged as the new Senior Prefect.

At the end of the session the atmosphere was lively and everybody was eager to see their final result, talo and Bose were together, Bose was optimistic that Tayo will surely emerged as the new Senior Prefect, immediately they release the result and be the overall best result the position was sure for him by the time result was pasted Tola has 71% and Lucky has 70% Tola and Bose were over joyed they said to themselves dream comes true, Lucky was so sad and his friend was also with him to console him, they concluded that he was the Press Club President, presently he should not worry himself, but the highest office was in his mind.

When the school vacated everybody went home for the long vacation holiday, Tola and Bose were extremely happy for their new status Bose was also the best overall candidate in senior secondary school II, Talo's parent was happy to saw the result of their child who emerged as the best student also awaiting Senior Prefect, they congratulate him in advance. Bose also told her parent about her new status as the best student in **SSSII**. She also told them about Tola new position, when Talo visited them they also congratulate him and prayed for both of them for more success in life. They both enjoyed their holiday, Dr. Oye took them on trip to visit some historical place in the country. It was a new experience for them they had a lot of journey.

Tola was excited and prepared for his new position on before resumption day. His parent also prepared for him.

On the resumption day. The principal Mr. Olorunosebi welcome everybody to a new academic session, he enjoyed them to work diligently and cooperate with each other's. The awaiting moment was drawing nearer when he got to the point of addressing the issue of prefects he implored the yet to be announced new prefects to abide with the rules and regulation of the school. They should also respect their fellow students and not to see the position as avenue to victimize anybody, they will be penalized. The principal said there was a changes in decision to choose the senior prefect and the changes was that the two overall students have the points that too closed to each other that was why they will not use it to judge the best, he further said that, management has met on it, and it has led to argument which brought about voting, at the end of everything Lucky Adams emerged as the new Senior Prefect. By this announcement the entire students was shocked and Lucky friends were jubilating shouting winner! Winner!! Winner!!! It was another sad day for Tola and Bose they could not say a word before they got home.

The story was narrated for the two family both Oye's and Ola's family there was nothing they could do the management has the final decision. They implored their children to face their studies because there was a brighter future ahead of them more success are still coming they closed the chapter and do other thing.

CHAPTER SIX

It was a convenient point for Tola in secondary school activities after he had lost the leadership position to his rival Lucky Adams by unexpected circumstances but, his leadership ambition continues to gear up in him. He passed out from secondary school, he was admitted to a University, and he has no problem because his scholarship with state government continues. Tola's father wanted him to study medicine in University that was he told him to enroll in science class, when he was in secondary school, but Tola settled for social science because of press club activities.By the time he was admitted to

University he quickly settled for political science as a course of study in order to pursuit his leadership ambition through politics.

Bose has already settled for social science class because she emulate Tola when both was in secondary school she has developed interest in Tola and also has passion for him, whatever Tola says was the final even to the extent that her parent cannot convince her on what both of them has concluded Bose was later emerged as overall best female student and she was the Senior Girl in her set.

Bose finally graduated from secondary school and admitted to the same University with Tola to study Economics as a course of study. Bose and Tola was very happy to be admitted to the same University, they continues their life and always support each other in whatever they engaged. When Tola was in 200 level he was chosen along with some student in his department to represent their department in student representative Council (SRC) but he was later screened out with unknown circumstances unknown to him. He later contested for Departmental President in his department but lost to opposition candidate.

This department election was proceeded the Students Union Election, immediately he lost the leadership position in his department, he went to students representative Council office to collect the student Union President form. After he collected the form he filled it and submitted it for screening. By this time around he was a 300 level student and Bose was in 200 level. Bose was later chose to represent her department in student's representative council (SCR) she told Tola to put his mind on rest that she will work for him through other members to be nominated as one of the constant for presidential poll.

Bose used her influence to support Tola his best friend to emerged as one of the students Union President Contestant. Many people collected the form but, it was a duty for (SRC) members to do the screening exercise at the end of the day Tola was chosen with another guy from Faculty of Arts, he was a law student. The battle was now between Social Science and Faculty of Arts, both Faculty now seeking support from other Faculty's to support their candidate to emerge victorious in coming poll.

Campaign has started everybody was lobbying for their candidate. During the student's Union election in

University every activities used to paralyze due to involvement of school management because they always wanted their anointed candidate to emerged, so that they can control the person to their own demand. Tola as the Social Science candidate and Sola as Arts candidate. They were two brilliant students that everybody likes in terms of good personality. Tola was gaining favour from others students because he was bold and vocal fellow who does not tolerate nonsense, this attitude was known to the school authority, they know that if Tola is emerge victorious he would be difficult to control for them. They concluded to support Sola as their anointed candidate, he was more approachable than Tola.

The race was began (SRC) has divided, because the management has called them but Bose Caucus disagreed with them. Management gave them money to support Sola and campaign for him. Bose causes refused to support Sola and campaign for him. Bose causes refused to support Sola because of Bose interest she cannot leave her boyfriend and support another person. When the show was getting tough, the school management was looking for way out to convince and divert the student's attention to their own side because many students prefer Tola than Sola and little the (SRC) members could do, even with the money given to them he cannot circulate.

The battle was between Social Science Faculty and Arts Faculty, more pressure on the students and management. They are looking for way out in the camp of management an issue was raised to suppress the students caucus, it was a Social Science student that always emerged as students Union Presidents other Faculty does not notice this, when this point was raised the students began to change their mind especially other department that has not taste the highest post in that institution. There was an argument among the students that they should allow other Faculty to do it, Social Science Faculty cannot be the dominant for life.

This nagging issue is the logic management used as a struck to break the back of the Carmel. Students has already divided, other faculty has now realized that, they were also entitled to the highest office for the students in that campus, it was now difficult to know who is who in this situation, everybody kept their decision towards their mind until the final day of election. The two candidate optimistic that they could win, Tola believe the majority of student has support for him and Sola also enjoyed the support of management. On the day of election everybody has prepared the campaign was over, the electorate has prepare the ballot paper and other materials for the election. At the end of the voting, the electorate counted it and the results was announced to the student, in their result the total number of votes was fifteen thousand two hundred and forty two 15,242 the valid vote was fifteen thousand and two, 15,002 Tola got seven thousand two hundred and twenty four 7,224 while Sola got seven thousand seven hundred and seventy eight 7,778. Sola was declared winner by the electorate. He was congratulate by the management and others students that supported him. Tola was so sad to the extent that he was rushed to the hospital for treatment, Bose also not happy with the situation because, she devoted her time for her lover to emerge but failed. Their both parents consoled them and told them that "Life is a double edge sword" which contained victory and defeat. Tola later graduated and posted for (NYSC) National Youth Service Corps. Bose was later contested for Vice President in her 300 level because the position was reserved for a female students and she won. She served as the Vice President in that institution with remarkable performance.

Please forgive me by Sola Olorunda

CHAPTER SEVEN

Tola was posted to one of the Northern State to served, he was there for a year, when he returned, the automatic work was awaiting him, and the State Government gave him job under the Ministry of Work. He was employed as the Assistant Director. Bose also through with her study, she was posted to one of the State in Eastern part of the Country for Youth Service Corps, after her one year Service she was also employed by the State Government in Ministry of Trade and Commerce, Department of Finance.

The sun that rise in the morning is a sign of hope for brighter day, the crystal rain drop in the season bring fact life in abundant this quotes synonymous to Tola and Bose lives they were fully employed and also enjoying starting their lives on a good note. Tola rented an apartment with a good furniture setting that can befitting the post of assistant director, he was always admired by his colleagues and ladies both in working place and his home. Bose was still living with her parent because they wanted her to move from that place to her matrimonial home. Bose always visit Tola in her leisure time.

In one brighter morning of one week end Tola invited Bose for a discussion in his house, top of the agenda was their future purpose. When the time come, Tola asked Bose a question. Who are you dating? Bose gaze at him which kind of question was that Tola? Since our childhood we had being a friend, have you ever seen anybody with me or have I ever introduced anybody to you as my male friend. You better go straight to the point. Tola responded, I just tease you to hear you own view, now that we have achieved a reasonable job we should think of settle down that was why I asked you that question may be you have someone else. But do you love me? And if you do are you ready to marry me, Bose responded my answered to that two questions was capital "YES", Tola was happy he cannot hide his feeling for Bose he embraced her and kissed her on lips.

Their discussion continues Tola told Bose that he was nursing an ambition of dabble into politics and he needs her support as a wife Bose said since you have been contesting do I ever against you but, we need to do something about the issues of failure or we should go and pray to it whether God does not want us to do it. Tola said this is what I trained for and I am being doing it is a matter of time. He later sighted an example of Late American President Abraham Lincoln who lost several time before he eventually became the president. We just need to pray to God for victory, Surely He will answer us.

Tola told his parent likewise Bose, both family held a meeting to finalize the marriage preparation how, when and where, the deliberation was concluded and the date was also fixed. Tola parent informed their family members so also Bose parent, likewise the young couple's do to their friends. The invitation was out, it was distributed to concern party, preparation was in top gear for the marriage ceremony on the introduction day, it was not an introduction per say because both family have familiar already they knew each other unless the invited people who does not closed to the family.

On the day of their wedding important personality from all walk of life was present including the top government officials who represent the state government official government because both of them were enjoyed the scholarship from the state government. It was a fantastic engagement in early morning of wedding day held at Dr. Oye residence, Tola's friend performed their duty by accompany their friend as a new bridegroom. After the closure of engagement they proceeded to church for church service where they were joined together as a newly wedded couples.

Pastor Ayeola was the one incharged of preaching to the new couple, he admonished them to do away with something that will chased them away from God they should move closer to God and put God first in all their endeavour. He continues by telling them that whatever sins they might have committed they should confess it and asked for forgiveness from God this will enable them to be succeed in life, failure to do this will jeopardize their effort in life because God does not want the death of a sinner but repentance, he later joined them together and blessed their marriage.

From church to reception where the final ceremony will be concluded, it was one of best hall in that state that was used for the reception, strictly by invitation the security guard was there to protect the government functionaries in that occasion. The reception was well decorated and designed, the chairman of occasion was the governor of that state in person of chief Dr. Oyato, after the introduction of dignitaries inducing both parents the newly couple's was later called to podium. There was a brief history for couple which they read to the people, in that short history is look like the bride has a successful outstanding than the bridegroom.

They dance and cut the cake and gift donation was allowed which everybody presented their own according to their which. It was joyous day for the newly – wedded couple, they were called newest couple in town, the both family enjoyed themselves and they were very happy to see their loving children married themselves at last, the couple were later board the latest car in town that was used for their wedding occasion which took them to their destination and preparation for honey moon.

CHAPTER EIGHT

After the honey moon Tola joined a political party in that state and be the active member of that part, there was an upcoming election in that state which every political parties was prepared to contest. Tola party was one of the foremost party in the state, they are the ruling party, and other parties are trying to hijack the power from them. They wanted to use every available means to get rid of the Tola's party.

In the party meeting, Tola was recognized because of his boldness and he was also a good speaker everybody liked his contribution. The election was drawing nearer campaign has started, other parties also doing their best to convinced the members of the public to vote for their party. Tola's party also doing their best to retain the power and rule the state for another four years. Bose was highly support the political ambition of his husband, she was always prayed for him for success as Tola has declared his own ambition even before their wedding.

During the election every necessary materials was available to use for the success at the end of the day it was a success outing for Tola's party they emerged victorious in almost all the post they were contested for. They won the Governorship election and they retained the power to control the state. It was a celebration alone for Tola's party they sang, dance and celebrate with all good things of life. Bose was also happy about the successful outing of his husband party. They also celebrate it at home.

After the swearing in of the Governor, it was time to share the others vacancies office by the politician, the commissioner, special adviser and other boards that needs committee. At the end of the day Tola was given special adviser on political matters to the governor this post to Tola was a stepping stone to realized his political ambition, he was in this post for the next four years which another election will take place, during this time Tola has gained favour from political gods father in that state because he was vast in thinking and always bringing brilliant ideas to move the party forward.

During Tola's reigned as the special adviser to the governor his wife always prayed for him for protection, she looked out and listen to people opinion concerning her husband she realized that everybody loves her husband contribution on political matters, this encourage her to support her husband it was the time for another election many aspirant has emerged for various post, as for the governor he cannot contest again because his eight year in office has lapsed, this gives room for other aspirant to emerged.

Tola informed his political god father that he wanted to contest for the governor of that state, they look at his ambition and told him to have more patience and wait for another time, they advise him to choose another post because there are many people who are looking for governorship position, he heed to their advice and settle for house of representatives members. Tola told his wife his ambition and what the elders advise him and what he has settle for in political arena. Bose agreed with him and pray for him she which him success.

During the screening for various post in Tola's party, he was eventually the ticket to contest for member of House of Representative. Bose did her best to campaign for her husband and other party member support him because of his political antecedent they campaign for him and also organized rally for him in that constituency everybody was aware of Tola representing them. The time of election was approaching, other political parties also campaign for their own candidate "it was survival of the fittest".

Election was smoothly conducted it was free and fair election which everybody agreed, but everybody surprised, all the post that was contested by Tola party was won expect the Tola post who narrowly loose to opposition party, this case who took to election tribunal petition, the tribunal judgment based on evident before them, they declared Tola opposition as duly elected candidate who won the majority votes, this judgment was not go well with Tola and his party, they took the case to court of Appeal after the examination of Appeal Court they delivered their judgment by upheld the judgment of election Tribunal who declared Tola opposition as the authentic winner of the Olorunesan Federal Consistency.

After the judgment of court of Appeal Tola's party accepted their faith and console Tola to leave everything to God they concluded that he has a good political career he can still make it in the future election. Tola has gained ground in his party, he cannot do without holding a post in the state after the widely consultation the party agreed to choose him as commissioner for works and housing. He was relieved a little bit but, the injury of his lost still trail him.

Bose was not happy with the situation of his husband despite the new position of her husband she realized that anytime Tola contested for any post he would eventually loose, she concluded to verify the ordeal of her husband.

CNAPTER NINE

Bose told her friend Bola about her husband predicament. Bola advise her to let them consult a man of God that can verify the situation. Bose agreed with her, they picked a date to see the man. On getting to that man of God Bose narrated the ordeal of her husband to him how the spirit of failure is tormenting him, he has contested for various positions in many occasion and lost by unspecified circumstances.

The man of God order them to let them pray, after the prayer the man said God revealed to him that, Tola had committed a sin which he need to confess and also asked for forgiveness from God without this he cannot overcome the spirit of failure the man concluded. Bola and Bose thanks the man for his understanding and accommodation, they departed from and leave to their various home. Bose was a little bit relived by knowing the mystery surrounding her husband predicament, she waited for him to through with his dinner before she narrated the finding she has made to him, Tola told her that, no one on earth can live without committed a sin everybody was a sinner and only God knows who is serving Him. Bose does not know what to say because she did not know any wrong things her husband has done in the past, apart from that they were grew together attended the same schools throughout their days in academic pursuance.

As a commissioner, Tola popularity continues to spread he was a committed servant who worked tirelessly to satisfy his people by meeting their needs. He carried out major work in that state such as road construction, bridges construction, and rehabilitation of some federal roads in that state, development projects in rural areas, youth's empowerment and better life for women. He was sent abroad in many occasion to look for foreign investors that can boast the economics of that state.

Some allied projects with other states were carried out by Tola as a commissioner which enable him to gained ground in some part of the country. He was a generous man helped his people for financial assistance many lives has been saved through his gesture he does not see himself as a only commissioner for works and housing alone, any urgent matters that arise from the general public, he tackle it without delayed. Tola was accepted by many people as a man of the moment.

Tola was a gladiator in the political arena whom his deeds convinced many people beyond reasonable doubt, they like him for his un-relent effort for the development of their state. During his stayed in office as a commissioner he was invited for a revival programme by her wife, they attended the programme together and during the ministration by the man of God, he pointed out that every deeds on earth there was a reward either good or bad, but confession and forgiveness was paramount in man's lives. Tola in his mind said to himself I have done a lot for humanity this is enough for God to forgive me on any sin that I committed so far we are all born to made mistakes, only God was perfect.

Tola tenure as Commissioner was finished and also the period of another election was approaching, he has gained ground to the extent that, even though he did not need to campaign before he could win any post for the sake of his popularity, both the political god fathers and other members of the party likes him for his excellent performance as a Commissioner in that states no doubt, Tola was not hesitate to open his mind as the next governorship aspirant for his party,   he concluded by telling the appropriate authority for his political ambition.

The gods father in Tola party does not hesitate to nominate him as the next governorship candidate for their party where the announcement was made to entire party members that the next governorship candidate is Tola Oye everybody was happy, he stood up and they clapped for him, he introduced himself and fixed the date for his manifesto which everybody agreed including the party executives.

Before the declaration of Tola as the candidate for governor there were other contestant in that party including the incumbent governor because during the screening exercise some were screed out and in the party primary Tola contested with the incumbent and won, even the election was just a formality because the political gods father has already adopted him as the party flag bearer for governorship post.

Preparation was in top gear for the election, in Tola's manifesto when it was read to the people they were all amazed to listen to a wonderful ideas from him, though they were not surprised as much because of his wonderful performance as a commissioner in that state. Everybody

was just singing, if we did not vote, you
have won. Our governor.

CHAPTER TEN

Campaign was all over the place for Tola as a governor even the opposition was afraid of him because of massive support from the people he was totally enjoyed financial contribution from the party members and other well-wishers, traditional leaders business men, captain of industries and all other dignitaries in the state are in support of Tola to be the next governor.

The only contestant that was given Tola tough race was Sola he was in opposition party though there are other eight contestant from other political party but, Sola was the major rival because his political party was the major opposition in that state. Tola knew Sola very well because he contested with him and defeated him in highly contested Student Union Government Presidential Election when they were in school.

Progressive Political Party which presented Tola Oye was the ruling party in that state, while United Political Party was the major opposition in that state, but the integrity and personality of these candidate can never be compared because Sola was a low key figure in that state, he was a grassroots politicians who was trying to contest in a big stage, his nomination in his party has brought a lot of controversy because some believe that Sola does not popular in political arena, with this, he cannot withstand Tola's antecedent in politics. But he was chosen as the candidate because of his manifesto to the party.

Tola antecedent can never be over emphasized because he had fame, integrity and popularity in that state, as a former commissioner for works he had won heart of many people in that state for his wonderful performance during his tenure, he touched lives and brought a lot of developmental projects to that state when trying to do the comparison of both candidate Tola has upper hand than Sola to win the governorship election.

The D-day was drawing nearer other contestants were doing their best to emerge victory there was not pushed over among them. In the day of election during the time of casting votes it was free and fair as adjudged by the foreign monitoring teams, the election was concluded and the result was being awaiting by the people everybody was optimistic that Progressive Party will win because of their candidate Tola Oye whom was the man of the people.

The electorate Chairman of the state was in the best position to announce the result for the people after it was verify by the part agents. The result was eventually released and United Political Party candidate Mr. Sola Olorunniose was declared as the winner with the total votes of four hundred and twenty one – thousand three hundred and fifty-one votes (421 351) which his closely rivalry Progressive political candidate Tola Oye who pulled the total number of four hundred thousand seven hundred and forty six (400,746) votes.

It was a shocked for Tola Oye and his Progressive Political Party when the result was announced even to the entire people of that state because nobody believe that Tola was not going to win that governorship poll. Bose was furious about the predicament of her husband and Tola later realized that if he did not confess his sin the spirit of failure will continues to trail him, he remember everything the man of God said in two occasions.

Tola later called Bose and told her, my dear wife it was now obvious to me that I cannot eat my cake and also have it at the same time, but I will explain to you how it happened. Do you remember your brother Wole the mystery of his death, it happened in that afternoon when you slept together, I came to your house and woke him up we started running around when we got to the pool side Wole fell inside the pool but I was in position to rescued him that day which I refused to do because I remember my parent constant warning and my humble background, my parent told me to work harder in order to get scholarship for my secondary and higher institution education which Tola was the only obstacle on my way because he was the best in my set that was why I leave him alone, he sank and died, this enable me to have the scholarship.

Bose was just looking without know what to say. Tola continues, I killed your brother due to circumstances in life, I now realized that no sinner will go unpunished, God has no son but reward, please forgive me!